By Martin Waddell

HARRIET AND THE CROCODILES
HARRIET AND THE HAUNTED SCHOOL

Harriet and the Haunted School

WEEKLY READER BOOKS presents

Harriet and the Haunted School

Martin Waddell

Illustrated by
Mark Burgess

The Atlantic Monthly Press
BOSTON   NEW YORK

This book is a presentation of Weekly Reader Books.
Weekly Reader Books offers book clubs for children from
preschool through high school.

For further information write to:
Weekly Reader Books
4343 Equity Drive
Columbus, Ohio 43228

FIRST AMERICAN EDITION

Library of Congress Cataloging in Publication Data

Waddell, Martin.
  Harriet and the haunted school.

  Summary: When Harriet hides a circus horse in the
closet at school, its nocturnal wanderings start a rumor
that the building is haunted.
  1. Children's stories, English. [1. Schools — Fiction.
2. Ghosts — Fiction. 3. Horses — Fiction] I. Burgess,
Mark, ill. . II. Title.
PZ7.W1137Hau 1985   [Fic]   84-71903
ISBN 0-87113-000-9

MV

PRINTED IN THE UNITED STATES OF AMERICA

A book for
MAEVE AND SARAH MURRAY

Contents

Harriet and the Haunted School

1 | Anthea Asks for It

"We've got to practice," said Harriet. "You be your mom, and I'll be you, and I'll show you how to do it."

"All right," said Anthea doubtfully.

"Here goes!" said Harriet. "I'm you, and I say, 'Please, Mom, may I have a horse?' You are your mom, and you say —"

" 'No!' " said Anthea.

"What?"

"I'm my mom, and I say No!" said Anthea. "I know my mom."

Impatiently, Harriet blew a bubble and

popped it. Some of the bubble gum stuck to her nose.

"You're your mom, and you say, 'Yes, dear. Of course, dear. What sort of horse do you want?' I'm you, and I say, 'A big one.' Right?"

"Wrong," said Anthea firmly.

"Why not?"

"Because I want a *little* one," said Anthea. "I want a little one to sit on, so that I can practice not falling off."

Harriet sighed and pulled the bubble gum off her nose. "All right," she said. "You say you want a little one and she says . . . she says . . ."

"She says, 'Where are we going to put it?'" said Anthea, who was beginning to get interested. Perhaps Harriet could *make* it happen. Harriet was GREAT at making things happen, although they didn't always happen the way she expected them to.

"You say, 'In the garage,'" said Harriet triumphantly. "A horse would just fit in your garage."

"What about our car?" asked Anthea.

"With your car," said Harriet.

"There isn't room."

"Not even for a little horse?"

"It's a big car."

Harriet thought about it.

"You could ask your dad to get a smaller one," she suggested. "Or ask him to get a BIGGER one, and put your little horse inside."

"It will have to stay outside," Anthea said. By now she almost believed in her horse, but not quite.

"It'll get rusty," said Harriet.

"The horse?" gasped Anthea, who had never heard of a horse's getting rusty.

"The car," said Harriet. "The car stays outside, and the horse stays in the garage. Right?"

"Wrong," said Anthea. "You don't know my dad!"

"What about in the greenhouse then?" said Harriet impatiently.

"No," said Anthea.

"Well, we'll think of somewhere," said Harriet. "I know we will. Let's get the horse first, then we can worry about where to put it."

"Mom will worry about that first," muttered Anthea as she set off after Harriet. She had to hurry because Harriet was a very fast mover. They were on their way to Anthea's house. It was called Don's View because Anthea's Dad was named Don, and he liked looking out of the window.

"I don't think this will work, Harriet," said Anthea.

"Why not?" said Harriet. She blew another large bubble with her special bubble gum, burst it, and stuck the gum on the nose of a nearby gnome. The garden at Don's View was small, and what there was of it was filled with Don's plastic gnome and Don's lily pond and Don's daffodils and *sometimes* Harriet. Harriet had been inside the house once, but she wasn't allowed in again. The insurance wouldn't cover it. When she wanted to speak to

6

Anthea, she had to tap at the window. This gave Anthea's mom a chance to hide things before she opened the door. She opened the door only if Harriet stood safely at the gate, and even then it took nerves of steel.

"Knock on the window, and get your mom to open the door," said Harriet, sitting down on one of Don's plastic toadstools.

"*Harriet!*" wailed Anthea.

She was too late.

"What a rotten toadstool!" said Harriet, holding up the pieces. "What's the use of a plastic toadstool if you can't sit on it?"

"It's meant for *gnomes*," said Anthea. "Come on. Let's go! Mom will be furious!"

"Nonsense!" said Harriet. It was time for action. She tapped on the window with a bit of broken toadstool.

There was a cracking sound.

"What a silly window!" said Harriet crossly. "It's no better made than the toad-stools."

"Oh, no!" groaned Anthea.

"It's only a crack," Harriet said.

"You broke it!" said Anthea. "You broke our window, Harriet! You've only been here two minutes and you've almost wrecked our house."

"I'll fix the window," said Harriet, and she peeled her special bubble gum off the gnome and stuck it over the crack.

"Your bubble gum looks sort of gnome-colored," said Anthea, inspecting it from a safe distance.

"It's only a bit of paint," said Harriet. Then she took a closer look. "And a bit of plastic nose!" she added.

"Off our gnome," said Anthea accusingly.

They both looked at the gnome. He wasn't exactly noseless, though he had less nose than before. Harriet's special bubble gum had acted as a plastic-nose dissolver.

"It makes him look more interesting," said Harriet hopefully. "He's nicer noseless."

"I don't think so," sniffed Anthea. She

loved her Dad's gnome. She had tea parties with him on lonely days.

"I know," said Harriet. "I know! Close your eyes, Anthea."

"Is it safe?" asked Anthea. She had a pretty good idea that it wasn't. But she closed her eyes all the same because she couldn't bear to watch.

"There!" said Harriet. "You can open your eyes now, Anthea."

Anthea opened one eye and then the other. She opened them one at a time because she had an idea that things might have gotten worse.

The gnome's head peeped out over a pile of daffodils, artfully arranged to conceal his missing nose.

"Dad's daffodils!" cried Anthea.

"Aren't they nice?" said Harriet.

"You've picked all Dad's daffodils!"

"Not *all*," said Harriet. "Only the nicest ones. I'll bet he's got more in the back garden, hasn't he?"

At that moment Anthea's mother came back from shopping. She saw Anthea and the broken window and the daffodils all at once.

"Where's Harriet?" Anthea's mom asked in a frightened voice.

"Here," said Anthea.

"*Where?*" asked Anthea's mother keeping on the road side of the fence.

"Here I am!" said Harriet.

"Standing in the lily pond," said Anthea.

"Am I?" said Harriet, who hadn't noticed the water around her ankles.

"*On* the lilies, actually," said Anthea.

"Don's garden!" cried Anthea's mom. "Don's garden . . . Don's daffodils . . . Little Don . . . what have they done to you, Little Don?"

"Who's Little Don?" asked Harriet.

"The gnome," said Anthea.

"He's nicer without his nose, don't you think?" said Harriet, catching on quickly.

"It sort of peeled off him when Harriet was fixing the window," Anthea explained.

"You almost can't see it's missing through the flowers," said Harriet.

Anthea's mom took a deep breath. She looked at Little Don, and Big Don's daffodils, and Big Don's toadstool, and the broken window, and the bubble gum, and then she closed her eyes and slowly counted to a hundred.

When she opened them, Harriet was lying in the lily pond.

"That rotten lily got tangled around my foot!" spluttered Harriet, uprooting it. A lot of other lilies came away at the same time.

"Go away, Harriet, PLEASE!" pleaded Anthea's mom. "Please, dear, oh, please . . . please go home!" She edged her way through the gate and up the path, heading for the front door.

"Go on!" Harriet urged. "Ask her!"

"Mom?" said Anthea.

Her mother froze, with the key already in the lock.

"Mommy?" said Anthea.

"Yes, dear?" said her mother, opening the door just wide enough to slip through without being followed.

"I want a horse, Mom."

"Anthea wants a horse," said Harriet.

"Only a little one, Mom," said Anthea quickly.

"To practice sitting on," said Harriet. "So she won't keep falling off."

"Mom?" said Anthea.

The door slammed.

"I think that that means no!" said Harriet.

"I think so too," said Anthea.

"She was upset by something," said Harriet in a puzzled voice. "Do you suppose I'm the cause again?"

"Don't worry about it, Harriet," said Anthea, who didn't like to see her friend sad.

"I'm worried about your horse," said Harriet.

"I haven't got a horse."

"I'm going to get you one," Harriet said firmly.

2 | The Horse-napper

"Horses!" said Harriet, pointing across Mitford Park.

"Those horses belong to the circus, Harriet," said Anthea anxiously.

"They've got lots," said Harriet. "They'll never miss one."

"I think they *might*," said Anthea.

"Which one would you like?" Harriet asked.

"You can't steal horses, Harriet!" exclaimed Anthea.

"I'm not going to *steal* one," said Harriet.

"Just *borrow* it, so you can practice not falling off."

"I don't think the circus will let you borrow one, Harriet," said Anthea.

"They might," said Harriet. "They might if I asked nicely."

"And they might not," said Anthea.

"I'm going to try, anyway," said Harriet.

All this time the Anti-Harriet Club lay quivering in the bushes, watching Harriet.

The Anti-Harriet Club consisted of Charlie Green and Sylvester Wise and Fat Olga and Marky Brown. They were anti-Harriet because of their experiences in third grade with her, and they were a club because none of them stood a chance alone. Right now they were quivering because they had almost bumped into Harriet on their way to the circus. Sylvester Wise had spotted her just in time.

"There she goes!" whispered Fat Olga.

"Where?" asked Marky, face down in the grass.

"Be quiet or she'll hear us!" said Charlie Green, who had hidden up a tree.

"I'm not going," said Sylvester Wise. "I'm not going to the circus if *she's* going to be there!"

"She's not going in," reported Fat Olga. "She's talking to the man."

"What man?" asked Marky.

"What ABOUT?" asked Sylvester Wise, who was the brains of the organization. He knew that it was "what about" that counted where Harriet was concerned.

"I've got a friend who likes horses," Harriet said to the circus man.

"Go away," said the circus man.

"I was just thinking," said Harriet. "I was just thinking that my friend wouldn't mind sitting on one of your horses now and then to keep it company. I think it would be a really good idea, don't you?"

"Eh?" said the circus man.

"My friend *loves* horses —"

"Beat it! Scram! Get out of here! You're in my way!" said the circus man.

"Does that mean no?" asked Harriet.

"Yes," said the circus man.

"*Yes?*" said Harriet, brightening up.

"Go away! Clear out!" said the circus man.

And so Harriet did.

"She's gone!" reported Fat Olga, who was first spy.

"Really gone?" asked Charlie Green.

"Absolutely!" said Fat Olga.

"Does that mean we can go to the circus?" Charlie asked.

"No way!" said all the others.

"She'll have let the lions loose," said Marky nervously.

"Or done something to the tent," said Fat Olga.

"Or *worse*," said Sylvester, who wasn't the brains of the Anti-Harriet Club for nothing. He was the brains because he was best at figuring out what Harriet might do next.

"But —" Charlie began.

"Remember the zoo trip!" said Fat Olga. "Crocodiles!"

"Remember the swimming pool!" said Marky. "All our clothes! We had to go home in towels!"

"What about the cement mixer?" said Sylvester with a shiver. "Remember that!"

Charlie thought about it. "I don't want to go to the circus after all," he said. "She could have done almost anything, couldn't she?"

"Yes," said Fat Olga.

"Yes," said Marky.

"She could have done anything," said Sylvester. "But it isn't what she could have done that worries me. She's *bound* to have done something, no *could* about it."

"What?" Marky asked.

"I don't know what," said Sylvester. "We can all go home or we can stay here and find out."

"I'm going home," said Fat O

"Me too," said Marky.

"I want to find out!" said Cha

"Then you're on your own
said Sylvester, who was far too sensible to
risk facing Harriet without having a mob
behind him.

"One for all and all for one," said Charlie. "Like the Three Musketeers, you said!"

"Don't be silly, Charlie," said Fat Olga.
"This is about survival."

With that, the members of the Anti-Harriet Club went home as fast as they could
and lived to fight another day.

"He said yes," said Harriet.

"He did?" said Anthea. She had stayed
well out of the way.

"I *think* he did," said Harriet.

Anthea's face fell.

"Don't you know?" she asked.

"I'm sure that that's what he meant," said
Harriet. "Well, almost."

"Almost?" said Anthea.

"He almost said no, but what he really meant was yes," said Harriet.

"I don't understand," said Anthea.

"I didn't think you would," said Harriet.

"What does it mean?" asked Anthea.

"It means he doesn't mind," said Harriet.

"Doesn't mind *what?*"

"Doesn't mind if we borrow one of his horses so you can practice sitting on it," said Harriet.

"You borrow it," Anthea said.

Harriet looked hurt.

"You're the one I'm borrowing it for," she said. "You *will* practice sitting on it if I borrow it, won't you?"

"Well . . . er . . . yes!" said Anthea. She really did want to learn not falling off, and Harriet was good and kind to think of helping her. She couldn't refuse, and anyway she didn't want to.

"Right!" said Harriet.

*   *   *

Soon it was dusk in the park, and in the

shadows only three things stirred. One was Harriet, one was attached to Harriet by a long rope, and the third was Mr. Tiger.

Mr. Tiger was a schoolteacher and a philosopher. He was the pride of Slow Street Primary School, though not of the principal, Miss Granston.

Mr. Tiger was enjoying his evening saunter through the park when something awful happened.

The something awful was wearing a Slow Street uniform, with a scarf pulled up to hide its face. He wouldn't have known who it was if it hadn't been for the whistling.

Mr. Tiger knew that whistle.

It belonged to Harriet. When Harriet whistled her special whistle, things came to her, all sorts of things. Lions. Tigers. Snails. Sheep. Tarantulas. . . .

Mr. Tiger shuddered. He could cope with sheep but he didn't like tarantulas.

"Hello, Mr. Tiger," said Harriet.

"Good evening, Harriet," said Mr. Tiger.

"Just having a little stroll, are you?" Mr. Tiger knew perfectly well that Harriet wasn't, but he wanted time to work out what she was doing and why she had her hands behind her back.

"Yes, sir," said Harriet.

Mr. Tiger moved closer. He walked around Harriet, and Harriet turned as he did, so that whatever was behind her back was still away from him.

"Harriet?" said Mr. Tiger. "What have you got there, Harriet?"

"Only a rope, sir," Harriet said, and she showed him the rope. One end was in her hand and the other stretched away into the dusk.

"Harriet," said Mr. Tiger. "Harriet . . ." And then he thought better of it. If he asked Harriet what was at the end of her rope, she might tell him, and then he might have to do something about it. Mr. Tiger knew better than to get involved in doing something about anything where Harriet was concerned.

24

"Good night, Harriet," he said.

"Good night , sir," said Harriet, and she called after him, "See you in school!"

"You look pale, Tiger," said little Mr. Cousins, the substitute teacher, when they met at the shelter.

"I feel drained." said Mr. Tiger.

"Not . . ." said Mr. Cousins, anxiously peering around at the bushes.

"Yes," said Mr. Tiger, and he told Mr. Cousins all about it.

"But Harriet is only a child, Tiger!" protested Mr. Cousins. "Surely we teachers cannot be afraid of a mere child?"

Mr. Tiger took a deep breath. "There are times, Cousins," he said, "when a man's got to do what a man's got to do."

"True!" said Mr. Cousins, who had the heart of a hero beneath his soft woolly sweater.

"There are times when a man's got to ask what a man's got to ask — like . . . like . . . 'WHAT IS AT THE OTHER END OF THAT ROPE,

HARRIET ?' " said Mr. Tiger.

"What was?" said Mr. Cousins.

"I don't know," said Mr. Tiger. "I was afraid to ask!"

3 | The Hidden Horse

"I've got it!" said Harriet the next morning on the way to school.

"Got what?" asked Anthea.

"Your horse," said Harriet. "It's a very nice one. You're going to like it."

"Where is it?"

"Hidden!" said Harriet, blowing an extra-big bubble.

"Hidden *where?*" asked Anthea, as they turned in through the gates of Slow Street School.

"Here," said Harriet. "I hid it here last night."

"In school?" said Anthea.

"That's right," said Harriet. "Hidden where no one will find it."

"But . . ." said Anthea.

"Good morning, Anthea. Good morning, Harriet," said Miss Granston. Her heart always sank when she saw Harriet. This time it sank even farther.

For Harriet was carrying a small sack.

Miss Granston knew better than to ask what was in the sack. Instead, she headed for her office and her herbal tea, which she kept on the premises for occasions such as this.

"Hidden where?" asked Anthea, as they turned in through the doorway of the third-grade classroom.

"I'll show you at recess!" said Harriet.

"Morning, everyone!" said Mr. Tiger and Mr. Cousins, breezing into the faculty room.

Nobody said good-morning back.

Mr. Tiger knew the signs. He turned around to go out again quickly, but Mr. Cousins was too quick for him.

"What's up?" Mr. Cousins asked.

"Tennis balls in my tuba!" said Miss Tremloe dramatically. "That's what's up!"

"Football jerseys in the kitchen dishwasher!" said Mrs. Barton.

"There's even a trampoline in the ladies' room!" said Miss Whitten, who had bounced on it when she least expected to and hadn't quite recovered.

Miss Ash didn't say anything because

she didn't know how to put it politely, but she had stepped in something in the auditorium, something that shouldn't have been there.

"Ah-ha!" said Mr. Tiger, who felt he ought to say something but who was far too wise to commit himself.

"Something's going on!" said Mr. Cousins, becoming interested.

"Something's very smelly!" said Mrs. Barton.

Miss Ash moved away from her.

"A very smelly foot, perhaps?" said Mr. Tiger, trying to cheer everybody up, but nobody smiled.

Miss Ash blushed crimson to the roots of her hair and went off to the ladies' room, where she tripped on the trampoline.

"Who can be at the bottom of it all?" cried Miss Wilson nervously.

"You know who and I know who," said Mr. Tiger.

"We all know who," said Miss Whitten. "It's Harriet!"

*　　*　　*

"Harriet," said Anthea. "Harriet? Can I see it now, before the bell, please, Harriet?"

"See what?" asked Charlie Green, perking up his ears.

"Nothing," said Harriet quickly.

"Oh, yes, there is!" said Charlie Green.

"Oh, no, there isn't!" said Harriet.

"Oh, yes, there is!" said Charlie.

"Oh, no, there isn't!" said Harriet.

"Oh, yes — ARUUUGLUG!" said Charlie as Harriet's sack went over his head. It had started off half-full of oats. Now the other half was full of Charlie.

"Anybody else want to argue?" asked Harriet, looking around at the rest of the Anti-Harriet Club, who had retreated to the far end of the classroom.

"There's nothing to see," said Harriet. "And no one is going to see it. Agreed, Charlie?"

"ARGLUG!" said Charlie, emerging from the sack.

"Does he agree?" asked Harriet.

"He agrees!" cried the rest of the Anti-Harriet Club from a safe distance, or what seemed like a safe distance anyway. There was no *sure* safe distance where Harriet was involved.

"Good," said Harriet, going to her desk. She removed the thumbtack Fat Olga had left for her to sit on and put it on Miss Wilson's chair instead.

Anthea sat down next to her friend.

"Harriet?" she said. "Harriet, you know the nothing I'm not going to see? When can I not see it?"

The Anti-Harriet Club held an emergency meeting behind the candy shop at recess. Behind the candy shop was the best place because Harriet was usually in *front* of it, eating.

"There *is* something," said Charlie

Green. "Harriet's hidden something and we ought to know what it is."

"Before she gets us with it," said Sylvester Wise.

"How do we know she's going to get us?" asked Marky.

"Remember the glue sprayer?" said Fat Olga, with a shudder.

"You shouldn't have said we could beat her if we stuck together," said Sylvester. "It only made her think."

"What about my Harriet trap?" said Charlie.

We fell in it, remember?" said Fat Olga. "Mud and beans and tapioca!"

"It was meant for Harriet," protested Charlie.

"But it got us," said Sylvester. "Harriet dropped us in it. She always wins! But she's not going to this time, not if I can help it! We've got to figure out what she's up to."

"What about the clue?" said Charlie.

"What clue?" asked Fat Olga.

"Oats!" said Charlie.

"Oats?" muttered Sylvester, trying to look intelligent.

"Oats?" said Fat Olga.

"Not much of a clue, if you ask me," said Marky, but he was wrong.

"There!" said Harriet.

"Where?" said Anthea. She could see where Harriet was pointing but she couldn't see any horse.

"In there," said Harriet, and she opened the closet door.

Lots of things were kept in the closet. Hockey sticks and ropes and balls and bats and the trampoline and tennis rackets and whistles and Mr. Tiger's deck chair that he used when refereeing matches. Lots of things, but today they weren't there.

Instead, there was a horse.

"Ooooooh!" gasped Anthea.

The horse blinked sleepily. It was a dreamy horse by nature and the closet was next to the pipes, so it was hot. The horse

was used to cold fields and parks. It hadn't been this comfortable for years, but it was still pleased to see its whistling friend. It nuzzled Harriet gently.

"There you are, horse," said Harriet. "Oats!"

The horse started to eat. It hadn't had a bit since last night's performance at the circus and it felt very hungry.

"Isn't it great?" said Harriet. "The gym closet is just right for keeping it."

"How did you get it in?" asked Anthea, looking nervously at the horse. It had big teeth.

"I had to shove it a bit," said Harriet. "Sort of sideways and around a bit and in." She paused expectantly. She was waiting for Anthea to say what a nice horse it was and thank-you-very-much, but Anthea didn't.

"It's big," Anthea finally said.

"Not very," said Harriet.

"I asked for a little one," said Anthea.

"It was the smallest one I could find," said Harriet, sounding hurt.

"And it's not much use to me in a closet, is it?" said Anthea. "I mean, I can't ride it in a closet."

"You couldn't fall off it, either," said Harriet. "There isn't room."

The horse gave a gentle, contented whinny.

Anthea, who had put out her hand to stroke it, stepped back hurriedly.

"You can sit on it in the closet," said Harriet. "You can practice sitting safely."

"What about exercise, Harriet?" asked Anthea from a safe distance. "Horses need exercise."

Harriet thought about it.

"You really want to ride it?" she asked. "Not just sit on it?"

"I want to ride it after I've sat on it," said Anthea.

"Up and down, jumping over things?" asked Harriet.

Anthea nodded. "What are we going to do, Harriet?" she asked.

"Leave it to me!" said Harriet, and they closed the closet door and hurried back to class.

*   *   *

Night fell on Slow Street. The pale moon climbed high above the water tower and stuck there, like a soft-boiled egg in a cup, and the only sound was the creaking of a door marked

MISS C. GRANSTON, M.A.
PRINCIPAL

as Ethel Bunch, the cleaning lady, crept through it on her way to clean the office.

Ethel removed the herbal tea from the filing cabinet, where it was filed under T, and settled in Miss Granston's chair, easing off her cleaning slippers and dropping them into her bucket. She settled her mop against the radiator to dry, and put her feet up on Miss Granston's desk.

The clock on the wall ticked softly

behind her, and as she sipped her tea, Ethel's spirits rose.

Ethel was dreaming of Robert, the Spanish mailman. He said he was Spanish and Ethel believed him, because he had dark flashing eyes and a charming accent. Robert had kissed her twice on Tuesday and he was about to do it again in her dreams when . . .

Clip-clop-clip-clop-clip-clop.

Ethel opened one eye, and then the other.

Clip-clop-clip-clop-clip-clop.

She closed her eyes. Perhaps she'd had too little sleep last night, but she could have sworn she'd heard . . .

Clip-clop-clip-clop-clip-clop.

Hoofbeats. Hoofbeats drumming down the corridor.

Ethel knew what it was, of course.

She had been born and reared on Slow Street, and Ethel's old dad had told her tales — tales of the Slow Street Phantom.

Clip-clop-clip-clop-clip-clop.

39

Ethel shrank to the floor as the sound of the ghostly hoofbeats echoed around her.

The Phantom . . . the ghastly headless specter that haunted Slow Street, hunting through the night for his lost love who had died of a broken heart in the farmhouse . . . the farmhouse that had once been on the site where now stood . . . *Slow Street Elementary School*.

"*Aaaaah!*" screamed Ethel, curling up under the desk. She stuck Miss Granston's wastepaper basket over her head. It was full of old exam papers and orange peels but Ethel didn't mind. Anything, anything to drown out the dreaded *clip-clop-clip-clop-clip-clop*.

The ghostly hoofbeats pounded past the door of the principal's office and faded away down the corridor, toward the gym, leaving Ethel pale and trembling inside the wastepaper basket.

Scooping up her mop and bucket, she ran barefoot from Slow Street School — into the arms of a passing policeman. It was a horrible experience for them both, because she ran with her head in the waste-paper basket and as a result she couldn't see in whose arms she was being held.

She thought it was the Phantom.

Ethel hit him with her mop, banged him with her bucket, and got arrested for assaulting a policeman in the course of his duty.

Within hours, the world knew Ethel's story . . . or if not the world, at least the staff and pupils of Slow Street Elementary School, where the Phantom still lurked.

4 | The Haunted School

The next morning, when Harriet and Anthea got to school, there was a big notice on the gate:

HAUNTED SCHOOL
KEEP OUT!

"Who put that there?" Harriet asked.

"I did," said Charlie Green.

"But I suggested it," said Sylvester Wise, who was too smart to go around sticking up notices himself.

"Does that mean we have a day off?" asked Anthea.

"Our school is haunted by the Slow Street Phantom," said Sylvester. "We are little children and we are nervous. We cannot be expected to share our classroom with ghosts."

"That's what I'm going to say," said Charlie.

"That's what I told him to say," said Sylvester.

"I don't believe in ghosts," said Fat Olga.

"People who believe in ghosts stay out of school," said Sylvester. "People who don't have nothing to be nervous about, so they can go on in."

"Then I believe in ghosts," said Fat Olga.

"So do we!" agreed everyone else.

The gate of the school creaked slowly open.

The crowd shrank back.

"Is it a ghost?" gasped Anthea, hiding behind Harriet just in case.

"I don't think so," said Harriet.

Anthea peered at it.

It stood perfectly still and it looked like Mr. Tiger.

"Are you dead?" Anthea asked.

"No," said Mr. Tiger.

"Are you sure?" said Anthea.

"Almost," said Mr. Tiger.

"Then you're not a ghost," said Anthea, coming out from behind Harriet. She liked Mr. Tiger. She didn't want him to be the Phantom.

"What's all this then?" said Mr. Tiger,

looking around at the bunch of pupils who had gathered outside the gate.

"It's a strike!" cried Charlie Green.

"Indeed?" said Mr. Tiger. "What's it all about?"

"The Slow Street Phantom!" said Charlie. "We are little children and we are nervous. We cannot be expected to —"

"GET INSIDE!" said Mr. Tiger.

They all went inside. Harriet went first, with the little ones, and the Anti-Harriet Club came behind her. They always kept behind Harriet when they could, for reasons of self-preservation.

"Didn't work, did it?" said Charlie Green, hitching up his book bag.

"It would have, if *I'd* said it!" said Sylvester.

"Why didn't you then?" said Fat Olga.

Anthea was last in through the gate.

"You are sure there are no ghosts, aren't you, sir?" she said to Mr. Tiger.

"One can never be sure of anything in this life, Anthea," said Mr. Tiger, stroking his chin thoughtfully. "However, if there are ghosts, I doubt if they will trouble us at Slow Street Elementary."

"The Phantom killed Ethel Bunch," said Marky. "It had great big teeth and scary eyes and it ate Ethel up . . . that's what Sylvester says."

"Scrunched her bones!" said Charlie Green.

"Miss Bunch is alive and kicking and out on bail, Green," said Mr. Tiger disapprovingly. Anthea's eyes had become as round as saucers and he didn't want her to be scared.

"But Ethel *saw* the Phantom, sir!" said Charlie.

"Indeed she did not!" said Mr. Tiger. "this school is NOT haunted. There is no Slow Street Phantom! Miss Bunch is unharmed. Her contact with ghosts was . . . er . . . strictly in her imagination."

"But sir!" exclaimed Charlie, who never knew when to be quiet.

"No buts, Green!" said Mr. Tiger, and

he stalked off to the faculty room. That was where he was heading, but he didn't get there.

"Help! Help!" screamed the cook.

Mr. Tiger dashed to the rescue.

"Blood!" cried the cook. "Blood everywhere!" She was standing in the middle of the kitchen, looking at the red smears on the floor and the horrid splashes on the countertop.

Mr. Tiger sniffed, and sniffed again. Then he dipped his finger in the blood and tasted.

"You devil!" cried the cook. "You . . . you vampire!"

"Soup," said Mr. Tiger.

"Soup?" said the cook.

"Tomato soup," said Mr. Tiger, and he pointed to the open lid of the large soup pot. "Looks as if someone dived in!" he said.

"Who has been swimming in my soup?" cried the cook.

Mr. Tiger didn't answer her. He had other more important business in the faculty room.

"Well, Mr. Tiger?" said Miss Granston.

"One strike settled, principal!" said Mr. Tiger. "A little firmness, delicate reassurance for the little ones —"

"Of course," said Miss Granston. "Well done, Mr. Tiger. That is the Slow Street spirit. Be reasonable, everybody. We'll have no more talk of the Phantom, if you please. We have our pupils to consider."

"Hear, hear!" said Mr. Cousins, who believed in rallying round the flag.

"There, there," said Miss Tremloe.

She wasn't taking part in the conversation. She was comforting Miss Ash, who had stepped in something-that-shouldn't-have-been-there for the second day running. It smelled like a similar something but it was in a different place. Miss Ash didn't connect the something with the Slow Street Phantom because there was nothing Phantomish about it. It was real and smelly and was located halfway down the main corridor, where Ethel Bunch should have cleaned it up, if she hadn't been otherwise occupied.

It was, of course, another clue, but nobody realized it, and nobody asked about it except Charlie Green, who said: "Miss Ash, please, Miss Ash, please!" when he met her in the corridor.

"Yes, Charlie?" said Miss Ash.

"Miss Ash! Why are you walking around with plastic bags smelling of perfume on your feet?"

"*Because*, Charlie," said Miss Ash, turning crimson with embarrassment.

"But, please, what for?" said Charlie, and Miss Ash gave him a detention for asking too many questions.

If Charlie had been given a straight answer, he might have told Sylvester Wise, and Sylvester, being the brains, might have added the two smelly somethings Miss Ash had stepped in to the oats and soup and come up with the right answer, but it didn't happen.

The working out was left to Harriet.

"I think it must be the two of us, Anthea," said Harriet.

"What must be?"

"The Slow Street Phantom," said Harriet.

"I thought it was a ghost," said Anthea,

who was still very nervous. She had been listening to Sylvester's version and she almost believed it.

"It was the two of us, and the horse," said Harriet.

"*You* and the horse," said Anthea carefully. She wasn't happy about the horse because she still kept falling off him. She had fallen off four times in the closet, and twice in the gym when Harriet got the horse out, and once in the soup. Even once in the soup was too much and Anthea wasn't going to risk it again.

"The soup was all gooey, Harriet," she said with a shudder.

"You should have gotten on again right away," said Harriet.

"I nearly *drowned*," said Anthea. She didn't want to drown. All she wanted was to ride horses, but if riding horses meant diving into soup . . .

"All right, I'm the one then," said Harriet.

"You haven't got great big teeth and

scary eyes and fangs dripping blood like Sylvester said," said Anthea. "Sylvester must be right because Miss Bunch told him."

"I haven't got my head in a wastepaper basket either," Harriet pointed out. "Miss Bunch didn't see the Phantom, she just heard it. And what she heard was the two of us."

"*You*," said Anthea.

"I'll bet she heard you falling off into the soup," said Harriet.

"I didn't mean to fall into the soup," said Anthea. "The horse dipped its head."

"He had to drink something," Harriet said.

It was the last class of the day and Miss Tremloe was in the gym, teaching Music and Movement to kindergarteners and twanging loudly on her guitar.

Little children waltzed around, waving their arms and being butterflies.

"Dance, dance, little butterflies!" cried

Miss Tremloe, twanging gaily.

In the gym closet, something stirred.

"Bounce, bounce, little butterflies!" Miss Tremloe called, twanging more loudly.

In the gym closet, something opened its eyes.

The horse was well-provided with the oats in the sack and a fire bucket filled with cold tomato soup that Harriet had considerately left hanging from a hook. It was warm and comfortable and feeling lazy, after the longest vacation it had ever had, but it was, after all, a circus horse. It loved music and it especially loved hearing the laughter of children as it galloped around the ring. Happy though it was in its cozy closet, its blood quickened as it heard the strumming of Miss Tremloe's guitar, and the sounds of the children.

"Twirl, twirl, little butterflies!" Miss Tremloe exulted, twanging even more loudly as she got caught up in the spirit of the dance.

The butterflies twirled.

The horse twitched.

Miss Tremloe twanged.

Twirl, twirl!

Twitch, twitch!

Twang, twang!

Twirl, twirl!

Twitch, twitch!

Twang, twang!

Twirl, twirl!

Twitch, twitch!

Twang, twang!

Twirl, twirl!

Neigh, neigh!

The butterflies stopped twirling.

Miss Tremloe stopped twanging.

"What was that?" she gasped.

Neigh, neigh! the horse repeated, impatient because he was missing out on all the excitement. He battered with his hoof on the closed closet door.

CRASH, CRASH!

"It's the Phantom!" cried Big Joseph. Big Joseph was the largest of the kindergarteners, and considerably brighter than any-

body else. He was also fed up with being a butterfly, and ready for some excitement.

"Nonsense!" cried Miss Tremloe.

"It's the Phantom!" shrieked all the little children, and they fled in all directions, including over Miss Tremloe, who went down in the rush and got all tangled up in her guitar.

"Help me!" cried Miss Tremloe, but her cries were drowned by the screams of the youngsters as they fled through the school.

"The Phantom! The Phantom!" they yelled. The sound of their voices echoed through all the classrooms. It echoed through the entryway as well, but there was no one there to hear it because the little ones had all run out of the school and down the street.

"Whatever is all this noise!" said Miss Wilson, opening the door of the grade 3 classroom and peering out.

"It's the Phantom! The Phantom!" cried the passing kindergarteners.

"Help! Help!" screamed Miss Tremloe in the distance.

"That sounds like Miss Tremloe!" said Sylvester Wise, who was right as usual.

"The Phantom is eating Miss Tremloe!" cried Charlie Green, jumping to conclusions.

"Aaaaah!" wailed Miss Wilson and she fainted away.

She fell backward into the arms of Charlie Green and Marky, who were ready to bolt out the door. They carried her out and down the corridor amid the fleeing hordes of Slow Street pupils, who poured into the playground and through the gates, anxious to escape from the haunted school.

"Harriet! Harriet!" cried Anthea. "Save me from the Phantom!"

"I don't think I can," said Harriet.

"Why not?" asked Anthea.

"Because *I* am the Phantom, remember?" said Harriet.

Anthea thought about it.

"Maybe it's a real Phantom this time?" she said.

"There isn't one," said Harriet.

"How do you know?" said Anthea. "Maybe there is a real one, with big sharp teeth and scary eyes and fangs dripping blood like Sylvester said."

"The one that ate Miss Bunch?" cried Fat Olga, coming up behind them.

"The one that chewed Miss Tremloe!" shouted Sylvester Wise cheerfully.

"You don't believe that, Sylvester Wise," said Harriet.

"I do if it means getting out of school," said Sylvester. "I believe in a great, big, scary, hairy phantom with goggle eyes and black teeth and talons dripping with teacher blood!" And he went around telling all the little ones about it, just to make sure they were good and scared.

All the little ones who were left to tell, that is. Most of the pupils had already fled. They weren't sticking around to be eaten by Phantoms.

5 | The Phantom Trap

The staff of Slow Street Elementary School gathered for an emergency meeting in the bicycle shed. It had to be in the bicycle shed because a few of them wouldn't go back inside the school.

"Snap out of it, Slow Street!" said Miss Granston. "My staff and pupils are too bright to be frightened by tales of the Slow Street Phantom."

"*What* swam in my soup?" muttered the cook.

"*You* didn't get twanged!" said Miss Tremloe, under her breath.

"Someone is causing trouble!" said Miss Granston.

"*Harriet!*" said Mr. Tiger.

"Why Harriet?" asked Mr. Cousins.

"Because it usually *is* Harriet," said Mr. Tiger.

"In that case, Harriet must be questioned!" said Miss Granston.

"Not by me!" said Miss Whitten quickly.

"Nor by me!" said Miss Tremloe.

"I'm out!" said Mrs. Barton.

"I quit!" said the cook.

"You can't!" said Miss Granston.

"I can!" said the cook and she did.

"Wait, please!" cried Miss Granston. Then she turned to the others. "Harriet must be interrogated," she said firmly. "If it weren't for my pressing need to straighten things out with the cook, I would handle the matter personally. However, in my absence, I call upon my staff to show the Slow Street spirit and cope!"

She went away to work things out with the cook.

"There is a way," said Mr. Cousins slowly. "The Slow Street way. One for all and all for one!"

Miss Wilson, who had been very silent at the back of the group, half-hidden by the lawn mower, crept away.

"What do you mean?" asked Miss Whitten.

"The Slow Street detectives!" said Mr. Cousins.

"Who?"

"All of us!" said Mr. Cousins. "We must band together and stalk the Slow Street Phantom in its den. Then we can prove that there is no Phantom, only you-know-who!"

"If we caught her at it . . ." began Mrs. Barton.

"We could expel her!" breathed Miss Whitten.

"I'm afraid I'm rather busy this evening," said Miss Tremloe.

There was a long silence.

"Thursday!" exclaimed Mrs. Barton. "I have my Girl Scouts. But any other evening . . ."

"I really don't think I'm free," said Miss Ash.

"I'm not either!" said Miss Whitten.

"I can't be a detective all on my own!" said Mr. Cousins, disappointed. "Isn't there any brave soul . . .?" Then he remembered Mr. Tiger. "Tiger?" he said.

"*Tiger?*"

"Oh, all right," said Mr. Tiger, although he knew in his bones he would regret it.

"We're going to catch the Phantom," said Sylvester Wise.

"Who is *we?*" asked Marky nervously. He was thinking about goggle eyes and black teeth and talons dripping with teacher blood.

"We is," said Sylvester. "I mean, we are. The Anti-Harriet Club."

"Being Anti-Harriet is bad enough," said Marky. "But Phantoms are even worse."

"Nothing's worse than Harriet," said Fat Olga. "Not phantoms, not vampires, not monsters . . ."

"It *is* Harriet," said Sylvester. "There is no Phantom. Harriet's it! And we're going to get her. It's Operation Anti-Harriet-the-Phantom, and this time WE'RE going to WIN! We're going to catch her at it!"

They began to plan. They planned for

hours and hours, because any plan to catch Harriet had to be Harriet-proof, which was asking a lot.

"Everybody know what to do?" asked Sylvester, grim-faced.

"Get Harriet," said the Club.

They slipped away from their secret headquarters behind the candy store one at a time, at four-minute intervals, going home by roundabout routes, using their Anti-Harriet Evasion Plan No. 3, the one with the book bags pulled down over their heads and the switched coats. When they got home, they started getting ready.

Gloves, to avoid leaving fingerprints.

Masks, to conceal identity.

Alibis.

And ropes for tying up Harriet.

"It had goggle eyes and black teeth and talons dripping teacher blood and it was hairy all over!" wept Ethel Bunch. "Oh, Robert, it was awful!"

"How do you know?" said Robert, the spanish mailman. "I thought you had your head stuck in a wastepaper basket."

"Sylvester Wise told me," said Ethel. "Oh, Robert, Robert, what shall I do? I can never rest while the Phantom still roams!"

"Don't you worry, dear," said Robert. "I shall go to Slow Street School this very night and unmask the Phantom!"

"Oh, Robert," said Ethel. "You are *wonderful!*"

* * *

Later that night, Slow Street School was silent.

In the closet under the stairs crouched the Slow Street detectives, almost ready to pounce. They weren't *quite* ready, because the closet was a tight squeeze, and they'd brought along their detecting equipment. Mr. Cousins had his butterfly net, and his flashlight, and his sandwiches. Mr. Tiger had spearmint candies and his tennis racket. Mr. Cousins got in first, then Mr. Tiger climbed in on top of him, and then they closed the door.

Meanwhile, the Anti-Harriet Club, boldly led by Sylvester Wise in a Dracula mask, had come in through the kitchen window disguised as burglars, and they were blocking off the corridors with food carts.

"And trip ropes," said Charlie Green, getting excited. "And the hose. We could use the hose and hose the Phantom."

"Stick to the master plan, Charlie," said Sylvester.

"What master plan?" asked Charlie.

"My master plan," said Sylvester, and he showed them their positions.

"We all go in front and you're the emergency backup?" said Fat Olga suspiciously. "Why do we get all the dirty jobs?"

"Because I'm the brains," said Sylvester.

Unknown to him, another Phantom-basher was at that moment dropping like a cat through the skylight into the boys' locker room. Robert, the Spanish mailman, would have landed silently if it hadn't been for his burglaring tights catching on a coat hook.

"Ouch!" said Robert.

He froze to the spot.

Had the Phantom heard him?

The Phantom had not.

Robert lurked in the darkness, pretending to be a forgotten overcoat, ready to spring into action at the first Phantom hoof-beat.

6 | The Phantom Rides Again!

"Hush!" said Harriet.

"I am hushing," said Anthea. "You're the one who keeps making noise."

"What noise?"

"Saying 'Hush!' all the time," said Anthea.

Anthea hadn't wanted to come out in the first place. She had had enough of horses after falling in the soup. She wanted a peaceful life, where she didn't have to explain tomato-colored uniforms to adults who wouldn't believe her. She hadn't explained it, really. All she'd said was "Harriet" and her mother had understood.

"Come on!" said Harriet, and they crept up to the fire door, which Harriet had unlatched before she left the gym.

"I'm coming," said Anthea.

"Coming slowly," said Harriet.

They went inside and closed the door. It was dark and silent in the gym, and there was no sound but a faint tail twitch from the closet.

"Harriet?" said Anthea.

"Yes?"

"I don't think we should be doing this, Harriet," said Anthea. "We're going to get into trouble."

"Only if we get caught," said Harriet.

"I think we ought to take the horse back, Harriet," said Anthea. "It was very kind of you to borrow it for me and I like it very much, but I think it ought to go back tonight before anything else happens."

"Don't you want to ride it?" Harriet

asked anxiously. Harriet had been working on a secret plan to please Anthea, involving her special bubble gum. Now it seemed to be coming unstuck.

"All right," said Anthea. "I'll have one more ride, just to please you. But not near the soup. I'm not riding near the soup again, not *ever!*"

"Ride it here," said Harriet. "In the gym."

"Just one little ride, then," said Anthea. "Then you take it back?"

"If you really want me to," said Harriet.

They opened the closet door.

"Hello, horse!" said Harriet. She whistled gently and the horse nuzzled her hand.

"What about me?" said Anthea, and the horse nuzzled her too. It was a friendly horse.

"Riding time!" said Harriet. "Sit, horse!"

The horse sat.

"It is clever!" said Anthea, climbing on.

"They learn it in the circus," said Harriet, and the horse stood up with Anthea on it.

"Oh!" said Anthea, but she didn't fall off.

The horse moved.

"I haven't fallen off yet," said Anthea in surprise.

"I know," said Harriet. "Trot!"

"Harriet!" squealed Anthea as the horse picked up speed. Then —

"I *still* haven't fallen off!

"I'm riding!

"Me!

"On a horse!

"Riding!"

Anthea went around and around the gym as the horse practiced its circus act.

"Wonderful, Anthea!" said Harriet.

Clip-clop-clip-clop-clip-clop.

"Give him a gallop!" said Harriet, and she opened the gym door.

The sound of the horse's hooves echoed down the corridor.

The door beneath the stairs opened.

The food carts began to converge.

An old overcoat in the boys' locker room unhooked itself and headed in the direction of the sound.

Clip-clop-clip-clop-clip-clop.

A dark figure appeared in the corridor.

"Tiger!" hissed Mr. Cousins, gazing at it.

"The Phantom!" breathed Mr. Tiger.

The figure came toward them and —

"Gotcha!" cried Mr. Cousins, swiftly

enclosing it in his butterfly net, brought along especially for the purpose.

"*Aaaah!*" screamed Charlie Green, trapped in the net.

"Charge!" cried Sylvester Wise.

Sylvester and Fat Olga and their food carts charged from one end of the corridor and Marky charged with his from the other. They all met at a point in the middle where Mr. Cousins was fighting Charlie Green.

74

"Stop! Stop!" cried Mr. Tiger, marching into the fray, and at that moment something came out of the darkness and attacked him with an empty mailbag.

Bang! Ouch! Crash! Bash! Whoom! The Slow Street detectives and the Anti-Harriet Club and their food carts and Robert, the spanish mailman, all met in the chaos, swinging and banging and punching and kicking and bashing and groaning and . . .

Clip-clop-clip-clop-clip-clop.

Still the hoofbeats came on.

Clipclopclipclopclipclopclipclop.

The hoofbeats came faster and faster and faster . . .

A great dark shape loomed, charging at the fight . . .

"The Phantom!" cried Robert, catching sight of it.

The Phantom came on at a full gallop.

"Nooooooo!" screeched Charlie Green, who had secretly believed in it all along.

"Save me!" cried Sylvester.

"Oh, *Mommy!*" said Fat Olga and she closed her eyes.

"Take that," said Mr. Cousins, delivering a straight left to a food cart. Completely absorbed in the fight, he had no time for Phantoms.

"Stop, O Evil One!" cried Mr. Tiger, who had seen a few horror films himself.

But the Phantom didn't stop. It didn't know *how* to stop.

It came on and on and on, charging down the corridor, and then, with one immense leap, it soared over them —

Clipclopclipclopclipclopclipclopclipclop clipclopclipclopclipclopclipclop . . .

"I'm on! I'm still on!" cried Anthea, but nobody heard her. "I'm riding!"

"The Phantom! The Phantom!" everybody else was shouting.

Suddenly the Phantom was gone. It had disappeared through the boys' door, heading for the open air.

"It was real!" gasped almost everyone.

"Oh, no, it wasn't!" said Sylvester Wise, who as usual had come out on top of the pile. "I know you all think it was the Phantom, but it must have been Harriet."

"Who?" said a familiar voice.

The corridor light went on.

"Did I hear someone scream?" asked Harriet. She was standing by the light switch, casually blowing gum bubbles.

"It WASN'T you!" gasped Sylvester, turning pale. "But . . . but . . ."

Meanwhile, the Phantom rode on, into the dark streets of Mitford.

People in its path fled immediately, without a second look. They certainly never got close enough to hear Anthea saying, "Stop, horse!"

And she said it quite often.

She said: "I can't believe it! I'm riding! Look at me!" and "Now, stop, horse!" and "How am I staying on?" and "Please, stop, horse, *please?*" but the horse wouldn't stop.

It was back in business, heading for the park and the circus ring and the sound of music and the laughter of small children.

The horse burst into the tent and galloped into the ring.

Around and around it went, around and around with Anthea stuck fast on top. She didn't fall off once.

"What a brilliant child!" cried the audience. "Encore! Encore!"

"Get off and take a bow, little girl," said the ringmaster. He hadn't been expecting Anthea and the horse to appear in the ring, but he wasn't going to be cross with a star attraction. "Not only have you brought back my horse, but you rode it like a champion!"

"I can't get off just yet," said Anthea. "I'm sort of stuck."

"What?"

"Wait till my friend comes," said Anthea. "I'll get off the horse when my friend comes."

Suddenly Anthea found she was a heroine. The ringmaster gave her free passes for every performance and lots of delicious treats and a special bouquet for being a star.

She walked home with Harriet.

"I stayed on," she said. "I stayed on brilliantly. I was absolutely fantastic, the ringmaster said. I was best-ever bareback rider."

"You were GREAT," agreed Harriet.

"You stuck me on," said Anthea. "Otherwise I'd have fallen off."

"I think you'd have stayed on anyway," said Harriet.

"What did you stick me on *with*, Harriet?" asked Anthea.

"With my special bubble gum," said Harriet.

"You should have told me," said Anthea. "I wanted to get off and I couldn't."

"Well, you're off now," said Harriet. "I only wanted to let you ride a little before the horse went back. I thought it was a good idea."

They walked on.

"I rode," said Anthea happily. "I really rode, didn't I? I rode in the circus. It counts as riding even if you are stuck on."

"Of course it does," said Harriet.

"I'm going to be in a circus when I grow up," said Anthea as they turned down her road. "The man said I could be. The man said I was brilliant. I could be a bareback rider or a lion tamer or a tightrope walker or —"

"How about elephants?" Harriet asked.

"Elephants would be great!" said Anthea.

"Right!" said Harriet. "See you!" And she walked away . . . *whistling.*

Anthea had a marvelous circus-star snack and gave her Mom the special bouquet to make up for Don's daffodils, and watched "Wonder Woman," and then there was a tap at the window.

Anthea's mother went rigid.

Anthea went to the door.

"It's only Harriet, Mom," she called from the hall.

There was a trumpeting noise and the house shook.

"Mom," said Anthea, peering around the kitchen door. "Don't be afraid, Mom."

"Tell her to go away," said Anthea's mother from behind the laundry basket.

"Mom," Anthea said. "You know I said it was only Harriet, Mom? And you know I'm going to be a circus star? You know circus stars need things to be stars with, don't you?"

"What is it?" gasped her mom.

"Harriet's brought me something to be a star with, mom," said Anthea.

"No!" said her mother.

"But —"

"Tell Harriet to go away," said her mom. "Tell her to take whatever it is with her. Tell her . . . tell her . . ."

"It's only a little one, Mom," said Anthea. "Anyway, she can't take it away."

"Why not?"

"It's sort of stuck," said Anthea.

"Sort of stuck where?" asked her mother.

"Sort of stuck in the doorway, Mom," said Anthea. "I sort of opened the front door and it sort of tried to come in, and now it's sort of stuck."

"*What's* sort of stuck?"

"My elephant is," said Anthea. "Sort of stuck in the doorway. Where the door *was*. The door sort of fell off, Mom, but it doesn't matter because Harriet's making a hole in the wall just beside it —"

"*Aaaaaaaaah!*" screamed her mother.

There was a loud crash and an elephant roar and a rumble and the sound of falling walls.

A plaster-covered figure emerged from the rubble.

"Harriet!" gasped Anthea's mom.

"I don't think much of the man who built your house, Anthea," said Harriet. "He did it all wrong. But it's much better now."

"My house! My home! Don's View!" cried Anthea's mom.

"He'll get a much better view with no walls in the way," said Harriet happily.